The Green Men of Gressingham

by

Philip Ardagh

Illustrated by Mike Phillips

You do not need to read this page – just get on with the book!

First published in 2004 in Great Britain by
Barrington Stoke Ltd
18 Walker Street, Edinburgh, EH3 7LP
www.barringtonstoke.co.uk

This edition first published in 2010

4u2read edition based on *The Green Men of Gressingham*,
published by Barrington Stoke in 2002

ISBN: 978-1-84299-222-7

Printed in Great Britain by Bell & Bain Ltd

Meet The Author – Philip Ardagh

What is your favourite animal?
A galliwasp
What is your favourite boy's name?
Fred (that's my son's name)
What is your favourite girl's name?
Heloise (that's the name of Fred's mother)
What is your favourite food?
A large portion (I'm greedy!)
What is your favourite music?
It depends what mood I'm in –
sad music makes me happy
What is your favourite hobby?
Collecting old books (not ones
I've written myself!)

Meet The Illustrator – Mike Phillips

What is your favourite animal?
A dog
What is your favourite boy's name?
Ben (my son's name)
What is your favourite girl's name?
Hannah and Olivia
(my daughters)
What is your favourite food?
Cheese
What is your favourite music?
Anything that makes my
feet tap
What is your favourite hobby?
Armchair cricket supporting

For Green Man,
an unsung hero

Contents

Robyn-in-the-Hat

Fidget

Friendly

Big Jim

Tom

Introduction

Meet the Green Men of Gressingham, a band of robbers and outlaws who dress in brown. Why *brown*? It's cheaper than green and hides the dirt better.

The leader of this band is Robyn-in-the-Hat. Then there's Big Jim, Friendly, Fidget and a lot more. They're going to take someone prisoner – Tom Dashwood, the hero of this tale!

Chapter 1

Up Before the Cock Crows

Tom Dashwood was up before the cock crowed that Friday morning. The servants had only been up for five hours when he came into the great hall.

They had cleared away the straw they used for their beds ages ago, and Cook had put some breakfast on the long table.

It wasn't normal for Tom and his family to have breakfast together. But this was not a normal Friday.

The day before, a big man had come to the Manor House. He wore a floppy hat that looked like a soft, round loaf of bread. His name was Able Morris. He had been sent by Tom's uncle, Lord Dashwood, to take Tom back to Dashwood Castle so that he could train to be a page.

In those days a boy had to train to be a page and then a squire, and then at last he could become a real, live knight!

Tom had been so excited that he could not sleep. He'd always longed to go to Dashwood Castle to train to be a knight. And now, at last, that day had come.

He'd spent a lot of the night thinking about mock battles. He could hear the

sound of horses' hooves and the cheers of
the crowds.

Tom's mum, Lady Ann, had planned a
family breakfast to say goodbye. This way
she could spend a little more time with her
son before he left. She was happy for *him*
but sad to see him go. Most mums are like
that.

Everyone drank beer for breakfast. They never drank water from their well because it was a horrid, brown colour and tasted like mud.

Now the day had come at last, Tom's mum wasn't hungry and her eyes were red. She'd been lying awake all night. She'd been thinking of her little boy Tom who had to leave home.

"Let's drink to my son," said Tom's dad, Sir Simon, rising to his feet. "To Tom, as he sets out to win honour and glory!"

"Honour and glory," Able Morris said after him, and everyone lifted their goblets to their lips. Tom felt so proud that his face glowed bright red.

"We must say goodbye now, Sir Simon," said Able Morris. "Tom and I have a long way to go."

Everyone, even the servants, went to see Tom off.

Lady Ann's hanky was wet with tears. "Be brave and true, Tom," she said.

Tom's dad gave him a hug. Able Morris got onto his huge horse, Ferdy, and pulled Tom up to sit behind him.

Tom hoped that they wouldn't ride too fast. He could not put his arms round Able Morris's waist. He was much too fat.

Able Morris turned round and looked at Tom. "Time we were off!" he said.

Everyone yelled "goodbye" and "good luck" at them as they set off to ride to Dashwood Castle.

Chapter 2
Gressingham Forest

At first they passed places Tom knew well. He'd been to them with his dad – the village, the church, the field where the Harvest Fair was held each year.

Then they were riding past places that Tom had only ever seen from far off.

When Tom looked back he could no longer see his home. All he could see was the very top of the church tower.

"We'll be coming to Gressingham Forest soon, Master Tom," said Able. "There's a band of outlaws in there. Don't say a word and hold on tight. We may have to ride off fast."

Tom was both scared and excited. It was only a day since he'd left home and here he was in the middle of an adventure!

Then the road went into the thick forest. Tom's mouth went dry as Able Morris gave Ferdy a kick.

On they went, on and on, deep into the forest.

Tom kept looking from left to right. The trees and bushes were dark and thick. *Outlaws and robbers won't bother with us*, he thought to himself. *They only want to attack rich people with jewels or bags of gold.*

He was wrong!

There was a sound in front of them. It was like the hoot of an owl, but owls don't hoot in the daytime. It must be a signal!

It was. Next moment a band of men dressed in brown was standing round them.

The tallest man Tom had ever seen came up to them.

"We have visitors!" boomed the man in a deep voice. "Let's make them welcome, men."

All at once Tom was dragged off the horse and stuffed into a sack.

The outlaws must have had some huge sacks, because they found one that would fit Able Morris.

He was a lot larger than Tom and he fought a lot. It took six outlaws to get him into his sack. They had to stuff his hat into his mouth to stop him shouting some very rude words.

Tom could hear all this going on, but he couldn't see anything because he was inside a sack too. It had been tied at the top with rope.

It was not a bad sack. It wasn't too thick, so there was some light inside. And it wasn't that itchy stuff that makes you want to scratch all the time.

Tom would have liked a pillow in his sack. But he didn't have too much to moan about – except that he'd been kidnapped.

If he couldn't think of a plan of escape, he might never get to be a knight after all!

Tom stopped shouting, "Let me out!" and thought he might have a little sleep. But then the sack was lifted up and the rope round the top was untied. The next moment Tom was tipped onto the mossy ground.

Tom blinked and looked around him. He was deep in the forest and the outlaws were all around him. They were armed with big sticks, bows and arrows. "Who are you?" Tom asked. "And what have you done with Able Morris?"

The very tall man laughed. "*We* do the asking," he boomed. The other men (for they were all men) laughed too.

"My name is Tom Dashwood," said Tom. "My parents are Sir Simon and Lady Ann Dashwood."

"So Lord Dashwood of Dashwood Castle is your uncle?" said a rather jolly outlaw. Like the others, he was dressed in brown.

"Yes, he is," said Tom with pride. "So I think you'd better let me and Able Morris go. My uncle will send out a whole army of knights to look for me."

"Oooh! I'm shaking all over," said the tall man rudely, and he grinned.

"Well, you're not brave enough to tell me *your* names!" snapped Tom.

"No-one tells me I'm not brave enough," said the man. "My name is Big Jim and we are the Green Men of Gressingham."

Tom looked round at the band of men. They were all sizes and they all wore the same brown clothes.

"The *Green* Men of Gressingham?" said Tom. Big Jim nodded. "Then why are you all dressed in *brown*?"

"It hides the dirt better," said the jolly one. "We don't get much time to wash our clothes. My name is Friendly."

Friendly held out his hand for Tom to shake.

Tom liked Friendly even though he was an outlaw. He shook his hand. "I do think it would be best for all of us if you let me and Able Morris go," Tom said.

"Not so fast!" said Big Jim. "What are you doing in Gressingham Forest?"

"I'm on my way to Dashwood Castle," said Tom. "I'm going to learn to be a knight."

"That castle is a bad place," said Friendly.

"For outlaws, perhaps," said Tom, "but not for good, honest people!"

"When were you last there?" asked another outlaw. The one called Fidget.

"I've never been there," Tom had to admit.

Chapter 3
Robyn-in-the-Hat

"We can't blame the boy for his uncle's crimes if he's never even been to Dashwood Castle," said Friendly. "I say we should let him go!"

Now Tom *really* liked him.

"And I say we should keep him here and ask for a ransom," said Big Jim. "Lord

Dashwood will pay well to get Tom back alive."

Boo! Hiss! thought Tom.

"We could do with a few bags of gold!" cried another.

"That's it, then," said Big Jim. "We'll keep Tom and we'll set Able Morris free. He can go and tell Lord Dashwood that Tom is our prisoner."

"We must ask the boss about that," said Friendly. The others said nothing.

Tom could hear Able Morris inside his sack, under a far-off tree. "I thought you were the boss," said Tom to Big Jim.

"Er, no," said Big Jim. "I'm only in charge until Robyn-in-the-Hat gets back."

"And Robyn is your leader?"

"Don't you know anything?" asked Friendly. "People sing songs about the great deeds of Robyn-in-the-Hat and the Green Men of Gressingham!"

"I don't get out much," Tom had to admit. "I've never been this far from home before – any new song takes ages to get to us."

"Well, you're a brave one," said a voice behind him.

Tom looked round to see a woman in an odd, brown hat come out from behind a bush.

"I don't think much of you lot! Not one of you outlaws saw me creeping up on you! I've heard every word you've said for the past ten minutes. What if I'd been a spy for Lord Dashwood?"

"But you're not. You're Robyn," grinned Friendly.

"So no harm's been done!" said Big Jim.

"So, your uncle is Lord Dashwood," she said to Tom.

He looked at Robyn-in-the-Hat. Her hat was very odd indeed. It was half hat and half mask. A flap with two holes came down over the top part of her face. Through the holes Tom could see two shining blue eyes.

"Why do you wear a mask when none of your men do?" asked Tom.

"They are full-time outlaws, Tom but I lead two lives," she said. "It helps us in our work."

"Why should I believe a word you say," said Tom, "when you told all those lies about my uncle—?"

Big Jim growled. "We are outlaws, but we don't tell lies about Lord Dashwood," he said.

"Dashwood Castle and its lands were once a happy place," said Friendly. "But not any more."

"There are all these unfair new taxes. Your uncle has sent out his Marshal, Guppy, to collect them," said Robyn-in-the-Hat. "The poor people who work on your uncle's lands cannot pay them."

Tom didn't know what to think. Why would Robyn and the Green Men of Gressingham lie to him?

"Dashwood Castle's dungeon is full of good, honest people who've tried to stand up to your uncle," Robyn told Tom.

"Able Morris didn't tell me any of this," said Tom.

"Well, he's your uncle's man, isn't he?" said Robyn.

Then there was another hoot, just like the first one. Big Jim put his huge hand over Tom's mouth.

Fidget pressed the tip of his sword against Able Morris's sack. "Stay silent or you'll be sorry," he hissed.

So Able Morris was silent for the first time since he'd been taken prisoner.

Now every Green Man of Gressingham was armed and ready. Who was coming?

Robyn-in-the-Hat and her band of outlaws were amazed to see a man on a donkey. He had been hurt.

"It's Max the Miller!" cried Friendly, and he rushed forward to help the man down from the donkey.

"What's the matter, Max?" asked Robyn.

"Lord Dashwood's men came asking for more money," the miller told her. "When I said I had nothing left, they said they'd take Gee-Gee from me." The miller gave a big groan.

"Does he mean his horse?" said Tom in horror.

"No, his *daughter*," hissed Big Jim. "They have odd names in Max the Miller's family!"

Tom was amazed.

"I tried to stop them," said Max.

"I'm sure you did your best," said Robyn.

"There were just too many of them," said the miller.

"You must have a rest," said Robyn.

"But what about Gee-Gee?" said the miller. He tried to sit up but it was too painful, and he lay down again.

"Don't worry," said Robyn. "We'll get Gee-Gee back, safe and well."

Max the Miller looked up at Big Jim, who nodded. "Robyn-in-the-Hat has given her word, Max," he said. "So it will be done."

Just then another Green Man of Gressingham arrived. He was dressed as a monk and had a large, leather bag.

"What kept you, Physic?" Robyn demanded. "Max is hurt. His cuts need to be looked at."

"And I need to see what I am doing," said Physic. "Bring me a light."

Robyn took Tom by the arm. "*Now* do you believe us?" she said.

"Well – yes," said Tom. But he still found it hard to think of his uncle as an evil man.

All his life Tom had heard such grand stories about his uncle.

Now that the time had come at last for Tom to train to be a knight he'd found out that his uncle was an evil man!

"This must come as a big shock to you," said Robyn.

"Yes," said Tom. "But how will you rescue Gee-Gee?"

"Are you going to help us?" asked Robyn.

"Me?" said Tom. "How can I help you?"

"The men at the castle expect to see you and Able Morris," Robyn told him. "If one or *two* of my Green Men can pretend to be Able Morris, and if you don't give us away—"

"Then I can try and free Gee-Gee as soon as I'm inside!" cried Tom.

"Not just Gee-Gee," said Robyn. "You could let us in and we could attack Dashwood Castle and set everyone free! It would save a lot of time if you could open the gate for us."

Tom felt a bit sick. "I'd like to help," he said, "but it seems wrong to open the gate and betray my uncle." What had his mum said? *Be brave and true.*

"I know how you feel," said Robyn, "but you saw what they did to Max the Miller.

He's just one of hundreds who have been harmed by your uncle's men."

"Can I give you my answer in the morning?" asked Tom. He was very tired.

"Do you give me your word you won't try to escape?"

"I do," said Tom.

"Then you may tell me in the morning whether you will help us free Gee-Gee and the others," said Robyn.

Tom nodded.

After supper, the outlaws sang songs around the campfire in hushed voices. Tom soon went to sleep. He woke up when someone put a hand over his mouth. In the darkness, Tom could just see that it was Able Morris.

"We must run away," he told Tom. "Come with me!"

Tom gave a groan. He had given Robyn his word. *What was he to do now?*

Chapter 4

To the Castle!

Tom looked at Able Morris. "I can't," he told him.

"Can't what?" asked Able Morris.

"Run away."

"Why?" asked Able Morris. He looked upset. "Are you in pain? Have the outlaws hurt you in any way?"

Tom shook his head. "No," he hissed. "But I've given Robyn-in-the-Hat my word that I won't try to escape."

"And I've given your uncle my word that I will bring you safely to Dashwood Castle," said Able Morris.

"Oh dear," said Tom, "we're both in a mess then."

Able nodded at Tom and crept off to the edge of the camp.

Tom knew he must follow. The sleeping outlaws could not hear them now.

"Let me think," said Able in a hushed voice.

Who should Tom trust? Robyn-in-the-Hat or Able Morris? Was Able hiding the truth from him? Was his uncle really an evil man?

"I know how you can get away from here without breaking your promise!" hissed Able Morris.

"How?" asked Tom.

"I shall take you prisoner!" grinned Able. Then, for the second time in 24 hours, Tom found himself in a sack! This time there was a gag in his mouth so he couldn't cry out.

Able Morris must have stolen back his own horse. It was the first thing Tom saw hours later. He had been let out of the sack and was lying on the ground with the blue sky above him.

"I'm not sure if I should thank you or shout at you!" said Tom to Able Morris.

"This way, you kept your word to Robyn," said Able Morris. "You didn't run away. I took you away from the camp against your will."

"But *they* don't know that," Tom said as he stood up. He sounded unhappy. "Where are we?"

"Look behind you," said Able.

Tom turned round and there was Dashwood Castle. It was even grander than in his dreams. It had high walls of thick stone, with a round tower at each corner. There was a moat of black water around it, and there were armed soldiers keeping watch.

Tom gazed at it. So this was Dashwood Castle, and *he* was a Dashwood!

He felt very proud. But what had Robyn-in-the-Hat told him? And then there was poor Max the Miller. He would ask his uncle about all this as soon as possible. Tom was very excited. "Can we go inside?" he asked.

"That's why we're here," grinned Able Morris. He got up onto Ferdy and pulled Tom up after him. They rode over a bridge that led to a small outer tower, where they were met by a guard.

"Halt! Who goes there?" asked the guard.

Marshal warned me about these two

"Able Morris and Master Tom Dashwood," said Able. His face broke into a grin. "Let us pass, there's a good chap."

"You may enter," said the guard, but he did not smile. He gave a signal to the guards at the main gate of the castle.

There was a grating noise and the drawbridge came down. They rode across it and through the gateway into the courtyard. Able Morris and Tom had got there at last.

Tom slid off Ferdy and at once a tall, thin man in a dark-blue cloak came into the courtyard. "Why did you take so long getting here?" he wanted to know.

"We were kidnapped by outlaws, Marshal," said Able Morris. He sounded nervous. "But we escaped."

The Marshal stared at Able Morris. "So that's your story," he said. "Bring the boy to his uncle. Lord Dashwood wants to see him and we must keep his lordship happy."

"Y-Yes, Sire," nodded Able Morris.

Ferdy was led off to the stables. The drawbridge was raised again.

"Are you Marshal Guppy?" Tom asked the man in the dark-blue cloak. Tom had expected him to be bigger and meaner, from what the outlaws had said.

"I am," said Marshal Guppy. "Have you heard of me?"

"Yes, Sire," said Tom. All at once he felt very small and lost in this huge castle with all these people around.

"You've heard good things, I hope?" said Marshal Guppy. He gave a nasty laugh. "I'm glad you are well after the bad time the outlaws gave you. Now, go to your uncle!"

****

Lord Dashwood was very different to Marshal Guppy. He was a big, round man and he had a big grin on his face.

He was sitting on a huge chair. His left leg rested on a wooden stool. It was bound up in bandages.

"Let me take a look at you, Tom!" he said. "You've grown into a fine lad!" He waved to Tom to come over and gave him a slap on the back and a hug. "Welcome to Dashwood Castle!"

"Hello, Uncle," said Tom. "We were taken prisoner by the Green Men of Gressingham! They said that—"

At that moment, Marshal Guppy strode into the room. "Time to take your medicine," he said to Lord Dashwood and bowed very, *very* low. He handed Tom's uncle a silver goblet. Lord Dashwood gulped down the hot drink.

"Thank you, Guppy," he grinned. "What would I do without you? You're my nanny,

my advisor, my Marsh ... Marsh-sh-sh ..."
His eyes closed and he fell fast asleep.

"You must let his lordship sleep now," said
the Marshal. "He's a sick man. Able Morris,
show the lad to his room." Marshal Guppy
picked up the empty goblet and left the
room.

"My uncle's ill? Why didn't you tell me
this, Able?" Tom asked.

"Orders," said Able Morris. "Lord
Dashwood's in charge of the lives of all the
people for miles around. He doesn't want
them to think he's weak and can't look
after them or give them orders."

"What's wrong with him?" asked Tom.

"He hurt his foot when he was out
hunting. Since then, he has never been
strong. He spends his time here in his
room. Sometimes he sleeps all day. It's the

medicine that does it. I spend my time here with him. That's why he needs Marshal Guppy to take charge of things for him."

"And does Marshal Guppy do what my uncle wants?" Tom asked.

"What do you mean?" asked Able. He took a large blanket and tucked it round Lord Dashwood.

"Well, it sounds as if Guppy can do what he likes, and tell people it's my uncle's orders – if the people don't like it, they blame my uncle!"

"That's not true!" said Able Morris. "I'd know if there were odd things going on."

"*Would* you know? You spend all your time in here with my uncle. You don't know what goes on in the villages or down in the dungeons."

"Well, then – why did the Marshal take the risk of sending me off to bring you here? On the way I might have seen or heard something that he didn't want me to know about. Why didn't he send one of the guards?"

"Was it Marshal Guppy or my uncle who asked you to fetch me here?" asked Tom.

"Your uncle—"

"And Marshal Guppy wants my uncle to think that everything he wants done, *is* done. So *you* had to go and fetch me," Tom went on.

Able Morris sat in a chair by Lord Dashwood. "I don't know what to think," he said with a sigh.

"If only I could get to the dungeons to find out if Max the Miller's daughter, Gee-Gee, is there."

There was a small sound, and Tom saw a shadow moving outside the door. "Someone was standing there!" he cried. "And he heard what we said! He'll report us to Marshal Guppy and then we're done for!"

They ran to the door. "We must act at once," said Able. "Let's look in the dungeons. If you're right about Marshal Guppy, we'll tell your uncle everything when he wakes up. Follow me."

Chapter 5
Time for Action

Able was a very large man – but he moved so fast that Tom could hardly keep up with him. They sped through a maze of passages and down some stone stairs.

Tom knew that he'd never be able to find his way back on his own.

"What happens if they won't let us in?" Tom panted.

"Then you must find a way to peek inside when the guard isn't looking," said Able. "I'll talk to him."

At last, they got to the dungeon. "Lord Dashwood has asked me to have a look around this place," Able told a sleepy-looking guard.

"Let me see your orders," said the guard.

"I don't have any written orders," said Able. "I'm Able Morris, Lord Dashwood's loyal assistant. I'm not a common soldier who needs written orders."

"Well," said the guard, "I *am* a common soldier and I *do* need written orders. And I'm not going to risk anything by letting you in—"

While the two men were talking, Tom slipped behind the guard's back. He went on down the passage.

There was a thick door at the end. There was a low window with bars on one side of the door.

Through the bars, Tom could see down to a gloomy room below. There was straw on the floor. It was full of prisoners. Hundreds of them. Some had chains. Some were free to move about. Men, women and children. Young and old.

They all looked thin and dirty.

Tom pressed his face up against the grating. "Pssssssssssst! Pssssssssssssst!"

"Who is it?" asked one of the prisoners.

"Ssssh!" said Tom softly. "Is Gee-Gee the miller's daughter there?"

After a while, a small, blonde girl was lifted up to the bars. She was crying. She peered through them and saw Tom.

"What is it?" she said. "Is my dad all right? Who are you?"

"I'm a friend," Tom told her. "Your dad is fine. He was hurt but Physic, one of the Green Men, is looking after him. The Green Men are going to rescue you all. Be brave. Tell the others that help *will* come. Robyn-in-the-Hat is on her way!"

Gee-Gee was so excited she gave a yell. The guard came running down the passage. There was nowhere for Tom to hide.

Tom didn't try to dodge him. He dashed right at him and then, at the last moment, dived between his legs. The guard fell onto the stone floor with a nasty crunch and Tom and Able ran away down the endless passages.

At last, Able led Tom into a room with a large, oak wardrobe along one wall.

They seemed to be alone. "Well?" Able asked.

"Gee-Gee and hundreds of other prisoners were there," said Tom. "What Robyn-in-the-Hat said was true. I know it's hard for you to believe, but you and my uncle have been tricked. Dashwood Castle is evil now. It's the outlaws who are on the side of good!"

"If that's true, Master Tom, then the guard outside your uncle's room, the one who heard us making plans, will have told Marshal Guppy. The dungeon guard will also report us. Soon it'll be too late to do anything. Marshal Guppy will lock us up too. He'll tell your uncle some story to explain why we're not there. Your uncle trusts him."

At that moment Marshal Guppy stepped out of the wardrobe.

"It will be easy to trick your old fool of an uncle," said the Marshal. "He sleeps most of the time, drugged by the medicine I give him. And right now I'm planning a bit of bad luck for Tom. There will be a lot of blood and broken bones. Take the prisoners away."

Two soldiers grabbed Able and Tom and dragged them off.

Chapter 6
Uninvited Guests

We often forget about one of the most important things they need in a castle. Water. Without water you die!

Dashwood Castle had a large well in a room on the ground floor. The water was as muddy as the water at Tom's house. They all drank beer here too.

That Sunday morning, something very odd was going on in the well room. Every few minutes a naked man climbed out of the well. Each man carried a sword and a sack. Out of the sack, he pulled a brown monk's robe which he put on. He then tucked his sword inside the robe and pulled the hood up over his head.

One man was huge. One was round and there were all shapes and sizes in between. Soon the room was full of hooded monks. When they were all there, the monks went out into the castle courtyard.

Tom did not know about the monks until someone looked through the high window of his prison cell.

It was Friendly, one of the Green Men of Gressingham, dressed as a monk. His hair was still wet from the well. "Don't be scared, Tom. Help is on the way!" he said softly.

"But you think I'm the enemy!" cried Tom.

"No!" smiled Friendly. "You told the other prisoners that help was coming. You're a prisoner in your uncle's own castle. You're a friend, Master Tom." He threw one end of a thick rope down to him.

Tom climbed up the rope and just got through the high bars of his prison. "What about the others?" he asked.

"Big Jim has freed the prisoners from the main dungeon. Your friend Able was there," said Friendly. "The Marshal's men only out-number us by 500 to 1!"

"We must get to my uncle and tell him what's been going on. We must get him on our side," said Tom. "If only I knew my way around the castle. I don't know how to find my uncle's room."

"Don't worry!" said Friendly. "I have a map." He looked at it. "Now, let me see."

Chapter 7
Attack!

Tom's uncle was amazed when Tom and Friendly woke him up. "Good morning, Tom. What's going on?"

"You've been tricked, Uncle!" Tom told him. "Ever since you hurt your foot and couldn't get around your castle and lands, Marshal Guppy has been doing evil things in your name. He's been over-taxing the peasants, and keeping the money for himself. He's also been putting good, honest people in prison – men, women and children, too. I saw them there last night."

Lord Dashwood looked at Friendly in horror. "Is this true?" he asked.

"It is, my lord," said Friendly. "I thought it was all on *your* orders until Tom told me what was going on."

"I must do something to put things right!" said Lord Dashwood. "Where is Able Morris? Is he one of Marshal Guppy's men, or is he still loyal to me?"

"He's *most* loyal to you, Uncle," said Tom.

"I'm happy to hear that," said Lord Dashwood.

"But Able Morris was taken prisoner," Tom went on. He told his uncle the whole story.

Tom and Friendly helped Lord Dashwood to dress.

"So the Green Men are here right now and are setting the prisoners free," said Lord Dashwood. "This is the perfect time to strike back at Guppy. I shall need your help, Tom. No more talk. Now – to action!"

Soon, the guards and servants were amazed to see his lordship walking around with the help of Tom and Friendly. They were pleased too.

In the courtyard, something very odd was going on. Some monks and freed prisoners were fighting with the castle guards.

The monks had thrown back their hoods and it was easy to see that they were the Green Men of Gressingham. They were all enjoying a good punch-up.

Big Jim picked up a guard in each hand and banged their heads together with a nice "THUNK".

The outlaws were winning.

But then Marshal Guppy rode into the courtyard with a group of armed knights.

"Kill them all!" cried Marshal Guppy, as he drew his sword. The knights drew their swords too.

"WAIT!" boomed a loud voice.

The knights stood still. They knew that voice well. It was their lord and master, Lord Dashwood.

He limped forward and stood on the stone steps of the chapel.

"STOP FIGHTING!" he shouted. Even the outlaws and freed prisoners stopped and stared.

"There will be no killing here today!" Lord Dashwood told them. "But someone may soon hang for the evil deeds done in my name."

"The old fool's gone mad," cried Marshal Guppy. "Why do you think I've been put in charge?"

"*I* am your lord and master, not Marshal Guppy!" Lord Dashwood reminded everyone.

Tom stood proudly at his side.

Marshal Guppy had made a bad mistake.

It was now clear that he had not taken his orders from Lord Dashwood. He had been acting on his *own*. The Marshal could see that his run of good luck was over. He galloped off towards the gatehouse. "Lower the drawbridge!" he yelled.

The guards did not know what had been going on in the castle. They lowered the drawbridge. "He's going to get away!" cried Tom.

"Don't be so sure of that, Master Tom!" yelled Big Jim.

Everyone rushed to the drawbridge and saw Marshal Guppy stop in the middle. Someone was standing there, blocking his way.

It was Robyn-in-the-Hat herself!

"ROBYN! ROBYN!" cheered the Green Men.

She nodded to the crowd and then, with a clever twist of her staff, she knocked Marshal Guppy from his horse. He flew off and fell into the inky moat. There he sank like a sack of stones.

"Where did he go?" asked Tom, running onto the drawbridge and looking into the moat. "Is he trying to escape underwater?"

Robyn-in-the-Hat dived into the moat. She was gone for some time. When she came up she was holding Marshal Guppy. They were pulled to safety.

"I can hardly lift him!" Robyn panted. When she took off his cloak, she soon found out why.

Gold coins fell out of the wet cloak onto the drawbridge. "He has gold hidden in there!" Robyn laughed. It was the gold he had hidden away in case he ever had to flee the castle!

Lord Dashwood walked onto the drawbridge. Able Morris ran out from among the crowd, and stood at his side.

"Hello, my loyal friend," said his lordship to Able, with a warm smile. "Glad to see you're safe and sound." Then he turned to Robyn-in-the-Hat. "Thank you," he said.

"I don't deserve your thanks. I'd like to say how sorry we are," said Robyn. "If it wasn't for Tom, we'd still think that you had given the orders for all those evil deeds. We should have known that you were a good man."

****

The next night there was a feast in the castle. All Lord Dashwood's friends came from miles around. Even Tom's parents were there. His mother was crying (for joy this time).

People who had heard that Lord Dashwood was ill were happy to find him fit and well. Physic had looked at his bad leg and it was almost better.

The Green Men of Gressingham all came. But where was their leader, Robyn?

"Who are you looking for?" asked a voice.

Tom turned and saw a beautiful, young woman in a long, green dress. She sat down next to him at the table. "I'm looking for Robyn-in-the-Hat," Tom told her.

"So you've met the leader of the outlaws?" she asked. "She sounds most exciting."

"She is," said Tom. "Her Green Men kidnapped me, but we soon became friends."

"Is she beautiful?" asked the lady, with an odd smile on her lips.

"She wears a mask so I've never seen her face," Tom had to admit. He looked at the lady beside him. She had shining blue eyes.

Tom's uncle banged a golden goblet on the table. "Let's drink to the Green Men of Gressingham!" he cried.

Everyone in the great hall of Dashwood Castle stood up. "To the Green Men of Gressingham," they cried.

They all lifted their goblets to their lips.

The lady with the shining blue eyes winked at Tom.

Could she be? No, of course not – but then again, she might be.

Friday Forever

by
Annie Dalton

Lenny has a crazy Friday, messing about at school. He wishes it could be Friday forever. When he wakes up the next morning, it's Friday again ... and again ... and again. Can Lenny escape?

You can order *Friday Forever 4u2read edition* from our website at www.barringtonstoke.co.uk

Problems with a Python

by
Jeremy Strong

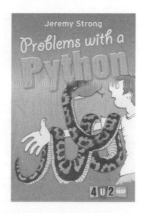

Adam's got a problem and it's out of control!
A snake has escaped. It's loose in the school
and it's Adam's fault! Can he find it before
things get wildly out of hand?

You can order *Problems with a Python 4u2read edition* from
our website at www.barringtonstoke.co.uk

Wartman

by
Michael Morpurgo

A wart starts small and grows bigger ...
Dilly's got a wart and everyone's seen it.
Now they call him Wartman and tease him.
Dilly doesn't know what to do – until he
meets old Mr Ben and everything changes!

You can order *Wartman 4u2read edition* from our website
at www.barringtonstoke.co.uk